How to Use the Viewer

light
source   wheel   eyepiece

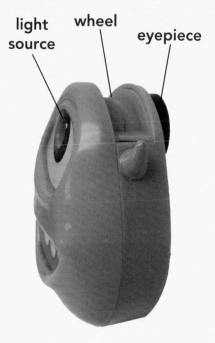

- When using the viewer, go to a brightly lit room or a window. Hold the viewer up to the light or window and look through the eyepiece to see the pictures. When using the viewer, do not look directly at the sun.

- Look through the eyepiece and turn the wheel until you find the picture labeled with a 5. Now you are ready to start reading Book Three.

- The numbers next to the text in the book correspond with the numbers on the pictures in the viewer.

- Turn the wheel to the right as you read through the story to see the pictures in order.

- On some of the pages in the book, the images are in 3-D. When you see this icon **3-D** put on your 3-D glasses to see the pictures.

Disney · PIXAR

MONSTERS UNIVERSITY

Book Three:
Scare Time

adapted by Susan Amerikaner

illustrated by Disney Storybook Artists

3-D images by Pinsharp

Reader's
Digest
Children's Books®

New York, New York • Montréal, Québec • Bath, United Kingdom

It was the final event. Each player had to go inside the simulator, scare a robot child and collect screams. Scare simulators were set to the highest difficulty level: HARD. The RORs took the lead, but after Sulley's scare, the score was tied.

It came down to the final two: Mike against Johnny. Johnny almost filled his scream can. Then it was up to Mike.

5   Mike's scare filled his team's scream can to the top. The OKs won the Scare Games. Mike was their hero!

    After everyone left, Mike walked back into the simulator. Sulley followed him. Mike gave the robot a playful, "Boo!" The robot screamed as loudly as before. This seemed strange to Mike. He looked closely and saw that his simulator setting had been changed to EASY.

11

Mike asked Sulley if he had done this. Sulley admitted it. Mike felt betrayed because Sulley didn't believe he was scary. Sulley insisted he just wanted to help.

"What was I supposed to do? Let the whole team fail because you don't have it?" Sulley asked.

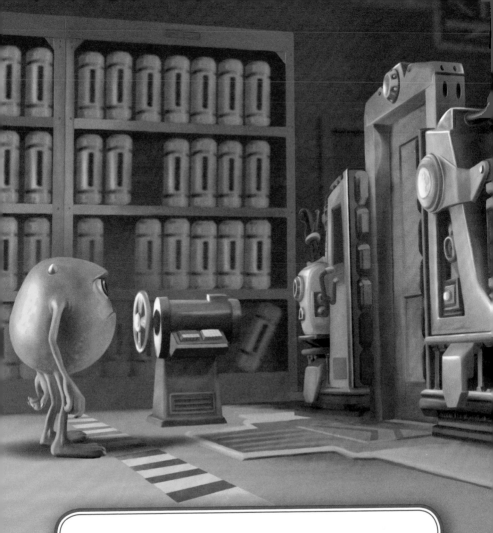

Determined to prove he was scary, Mike broke into the Door Tech Lab and activated a door to the human world. Meanwhile, Sulley told Hardscrabble he had cheated. She was furious. "I expect you off campus by tomorrow," she said. An alarm sounded and Hardscrabble flew to the lab. Sulley followed.

Mike walked through the door. He crept up to a bed and roared at a little girl. "You look funny," she said, smiling. Mike was stunned. Suddenly, he realized he wasn't in a bedroom. He was in a cabin filled with kids!

Back in the lab, Hardscrabble wouldn't let anyone near the door. With Don's help, Sulley slipped through the door and into the cabin. But Mike wasn't there—the cabin was empty!

He had to find Mike, so Sulley climbed out a window. The rangers chased Sulley, thinking he was a bear.

Sulley found Mike, dejected, sitting by the lake. "You were right," Mike said. "They weren't scared of me." Sulley said he understood how Mike felt. Mike snapped, "You'll never know what it's like to be a failure because you were born a Sullivan!"

Sulley replied, "But...I'm the worst Sullivan...you're not the only failure here."

Mike asked, "How come you never told me that before?"

"Because...we weren't friends before," said Sulley.

After a close call with the rangers, Sulley and Mike raced back to the cabin.

Dean Hardscrabble shut down power to the door, leaving Mike and Sulley trapped in the cabin. Sulley panicked, but Mike had a plan. If they scared the rangers, they might generate enough scream energy to power up the door from their side. His plan included skittering shadows, strange sounds, claw marks, low growls,

bunk beds falling, and tangling the terrified rangers in fishing line. Finally, Sulley jumped into view and roared his most ferocious, atrocious ROAR. The rangers screamed so loudly, every scream can back in the lab filled to the brim. The door powered up—and Mike and Sulley exploded back into the lab.

⑦

Sulley and Mike were expelled from MU, but Hardscrabble admitted the other OKs into the Scaring Program. She had been impressed with their Scare Games performance. For the first time, Mike didn't have a plan.

At the front gates of MU, Dean Hardscrabble met Mike and Sulley. "Well, it seems you made the front page again," she said. She confessed that Sulley and Mike had done something no one had ever done before: they had surprised her.

As Hardscrabble flew off, Mike noticed the help-wanted ad on the back of the newspaper. He showed it to Sulley, who smiled. So Mike had another plan, after all.

They applied and got jobs in the mailroom at Monsters, Inc.! That was how Team Wazowski and Sullivan began their long and successful careers.

8